RAINBOW MAGIC:
MELODIE THE MUSIC FAIRY

First published in Great Britain in 2005
by Orchard Books
This Large Print edition published 2010
by BBC Audiobooks Ltd
by arrangement with
Orchard Books

ISBN: 978 1405 663861

HiT entertainment

British Library Cataloguing in Publication Data available

Melodie
the Music
Fairy

Daisy Meadows

Illustrated by Georgie Ripper

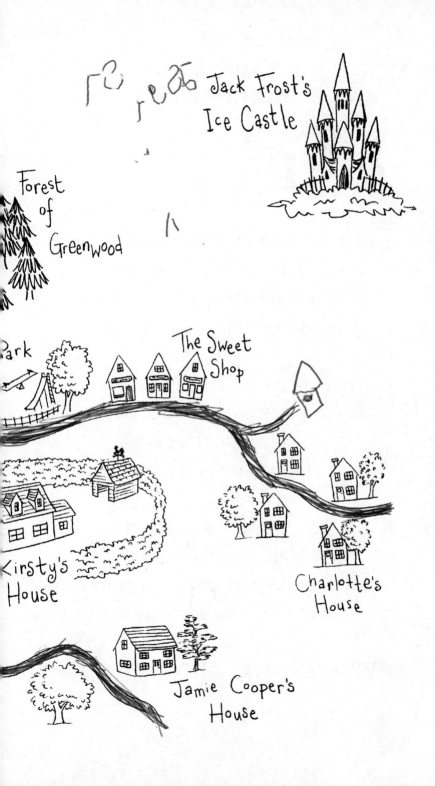

Jack Frost's
Ice Castle

Forest
of
Greenwood

Park

The Sweet
Shop

Kirsty's
House

Charlotte's
House

Jamie Cooper's
House

A Very Special
Party Invitation

Our gracious King and gentle Queen
Are loved by fairies all.
One thousand years have they ruled well,
Through troubles great and small.

In honour of their glorious reign
A party has been planned,
To celebrate their jubilee
Throughout all Fairyland.

The party is a royal surprise,
We hope they'll be delighted.
So shine your wand and press your dress...
For *you* have been invited!

RSVP: HRH THE FAIRY GODMOTHER

Contents

For Alice and Lara Clerc, with the
hope that they will seek out and
find lovely fairies in France.

Special thanks to
Marilyn Kaye

Musical Mayhem

"Kirsty, you're a brilliant dancer!"
Rachel Walker smiled, clapping
her hands as her friend took
a bow. Kirsty had just finished
practising the ballet steps she
would be performing later
that evening.

"It will look even better tonight,
with the other dancers and the

1

proper costumes," Kirsty replied
with a grin. "And wait till you hear
the lovely music."

Rachel was staying with her best
friend, Kirsty Tate, for the week.
That evening, the girls were going
to the village hall for a special
occasion – the first anniversary
of Kirsty's ballet school.

"It's going to be a great party,"
Kirsty went on. "My ballet teacher
is decorating the hall
and organising some games,
and all the parents are
bringing food."

"It sounds fun,"
Rachel agreed.
"But if it's a party,
then we'll have to
be on the lookout
for goblins!"

Kirsty nodded. She and Rachel shared a magical secret: they were friends with the fairies! But, right now, there were problems in Fairyland and Kirsty and Rachel had promised to help.

The fairies were planning a surprise celebration for the 1000th jubilee of the Fairy King and Queen. It was meant to be taking place in five days' time, and the Party Fairies were in charge of making it as special as possible using their party bags of magic fairy dust.

But nasty Jack Frost had other plans. Banished to his ice castle by the Fairy King and Queen, he had decided to throw a party of his own on the very same day. Jack Frost knew that whenever a party in the human world went wrong, the Party

Fairies would fly to the rescue. So he had cunningly sent his goblin servants to spoil as many human parties as possible, and grab the fairies' party bags when they flew in to set things right. Then fairy magic would make his party spectacular, but the jubilee celebrations would be ruined!

Suddenly, the girls heard Mrs Tate's voice. "Time to go, girls!" she called.

Kirsty and Rachel hurried downstairs to join Kirsty's mum and dad.

Mr Tate held
up a cake tin.
"I made some
cakes for
the party,"
he explained,
lifting the lid.
"Fairy
cakes!" Rachel
laughed with delight.
"You couldn't have made
anything better."

"Thanks, Dad," Kirsty grinned,
tucking the tin under her arm.

Mr Tate drove them all to the
village hall. They arrived to find
it already full of friends and
families who had come to join
the celebration.

"The hall looks so different!"
Kirsty gasped. Several rows of chairs
had been set up to face the stage,

5

just like in a real theatre. Shiny silver streamers hung from the ceiling, twinkling fairy lights bordered the stage and bunches of silver and white balloons floated above each table of food.

While Mr and Mrs Tate chatted to other parents, Rachel and Kirsty arranged the fairy cakes on a plate. The cakes weren't the only things that looked delicious.

"Yum, chocolate éclairs!" Kirsty pointed out. Then she frowned. "They look almost too good to be true."

"Maybe we should test some of these – just to make sure the food hasn't been spoiled by a goblin," Rachel suggested.

Kirsty nodded. She took an éclair and Rachel ate one of Mr Tate's fairy cakes. Then the girls smiled at each other – the cakes were

delicious, no goblins had been
anywhere near this party food.

Just then, the ballet teacher, Miss
Kelly, joined them. "Kirsty, it's time
for you to go and get ready now,"
she said. "And you
must be
Rachel," she
added with
a smile.
"Kirsty said
you would
be coming."
"Can I help
Kirsty and
the other girls
get ready?"
Rachel asked
eagerly.

Miss Kelly nodded. "Thank you,
Rachel. I could certainly use another
pair of hands."

Kirsty led the way to the dressing room, which was behind the stage. While the dancers slipped into their tights and tutus, Rachel helped Miss Kelly apply rosy powder to the girls' cheeks and a dab of pink gloss to their lips. Finally, the dancers put on their ballet shoes, tying the pink satin ribbons firmly around their ankles.

There was a feeling of excitement in the air as the audience took their seats. Watching from backstage, Rachel breathed a sigh of relief. The decorations, the food and the costumes were perfect. It looked like Jack Frost's goblins hadn't heard about the ballet-school party.

Miss Kelly walked onto the stage. "Ladies and gentlemen, I am pleased to present our very first class of ballerinas, who will perform for you tonight in honour of our school's anniversary," she announced.

The audience clapped as Miss
Kelly hurried into the wings.
Then the curtain rose, and
the music began.

With their arms held gracefully
over their heads, the dancers ran
daintily onto the stage. Having seen
Kirsty practise, Rachel knew what
was coming next. But she hadn't
seen the dance with the costumes
and music. She watched in delight –
the girls looked as beautiful
as fairies in their pretty, gauzy tutus.

But then, suddenly, the music changed. It seemed to speed up and the dancers started to have difficulty staying in time. Although they were dancing on bravely, Rachel could see from Kirsty's face that something was wrong.

She watched in dismay as one or two of the girls stumbled, stubbing their toes on the stage as they tried to pirouette more quickly.

The music was still getting faster and faster, and the tune was now just a squeaky jumble of noise. Rachel glanced across at Miss Kelly. Red in the face, the teacher was

frantically pressing the buttons on the CD-player, one after the other, but it wasn't making any difference. The  dancers whirled and spun, quicker and quicker, but it was impossible for them to keep to the beat. Two dancers bumped into each other, and another tripped over her own feet.

"I can't stop the CD-player!" Miss Kelly gasped. "I don't know what's wrong with it."

But Rachel knew. She was sure that this was the work of one of Jack Frost's goblins!

The Trembling Tambourine

The girls abandoned their performance, and rushed offstage to see what was going on. A couple of the parents came too, to help Miss Kelly with the music. But nobody seemed to know what was wrong with the CD-player.

"This is definitely goblin mischief!" Rachel said to herself. She looked for Kirsty, but couldn't see her in the crowd of people backstage. "Well, I'm going to find him and stop his tricks!"

Rachel glanced round the village hall, and her heart sank. She could see lots of places where a goblin could hide. Backstage there were trunks and racks of costumes and the big cardboard set from the last pantomime – not to mention two dressing rooms, a music room and a tiny office.

But then, just as Rachel was wondering where to start her search, she saw a pile of musical instruments stacked in the wings on the other side of the stage. And one of them, a tambourine, was shaking, all on its own!

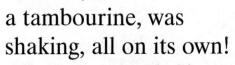

Rachel gulped. She could see that there was no one on that side of the stage, and all the other instruments were still. She knew the tambourine was too small to hide a goblin, but what was making it tremble? Could a goblin have brushed past it

and set it moving, she wondered.
And could the goblin still be lurking
over there?

As quietly as she could, Rachel
slipped across the stage to the other
side. She crept towards the stack
of instruments,
looking around
carefully in
case the
goblin was
hiding nearby.
She wanted
to be sure
to spot him before

he spotted her!
But she couldn't see anything
suspicious so, with her heart
pounding, she knelt down beside
the tinkling tambourine.
Very carefully, Rachel lifted
the rim with one finger.

As she did so, a golden glow flooded out from underneath.

Rachel grinned and lifted the tambourine away eagerly. She had already guessed what she would find, and sure enough, tucked away with her face buried in her gauzy skirt, was a tiny, shimmering fairy.

"You're a Party Fairy!" Rachel exclaimed with delight.

The fairy raised her head. She was sobbing so hard that she had been making the tambourine bells jingle. Tears like tiny diamonds rolled down her cheeks as she adjusted her little gold hairband. "That's r-right, I'm Melodie the Music Fairy," she sniffed sadly. "And you must be Rachel."

Melodie stood up on tiptoe. She was wearing a beautiful pink ballet dress, with black musical notes all around the hem. Her golden hair was in plaits that swung as she turned her head.

"Where's Kirsty?" Melodie asked.

"She's not far away," Rachel told her. "But why are you crying?"

Melodie wiped away a last sparkling tear. "I came to fix the music," she explained. "If I had known one of those nasty goblins had made it go wrong, I would have been more careful."

Rachel frowned. "Was a goblin waiting for you?"

"Yes," Melodie wailed. "He grabbed my party bag and ran off with it. Now I can't fix the music for the girls' ballet. And if I don't get my party bag back, there won't be any music for the King and Queen's jubilee party, either!"

Melodie's Mission

Rachel felt very sorry for Melodie. "Don't worry," she said. "Kirsty and I will help you get your party bag back."

Melodie brightened immediately. "Oh, do you mean it?" she cried eagerly.

Rachel smiled. "Of course I do," she replied. "Now let's go and find Kirsty."

Quickly, Melodie picked up her glittering wand and fluttered into the pocket of Rachel's skirt. Then Rachel made her way back towards the people gathered around the CD-player.

Kirsty spotted her friend coming across the stage, and hurried to meet her. "Rachel, I think I know what happened to the music," Kirsty whispered in her ear. "It's goblin trouble!"

Rachel nodded. "Look!" she said, and held her skirt pocket open so Kirsty could peek inside.

Melodie waved at her. "Hello, Kirsty. I'm Melodie the Music Fairy," she called in her soft silvery voice.

"Oh, Melodie, I'm so pleased to see you," Kirsty said gratefully. "If anyone can help us, you can."

"She came here to fix the music," Rachel explained. "But a goblin stole her party bag."

Kirsty's face fell. "Oh, no!" she gasped. "We have to get it back before the goblin escapes and takes it to Jack Frost!"

Melodie nodded enthusiastically.

"But where should we start looking?" she asked.

Rachel thought about this. "There are so many people in the main hall, I don't think he would hang around there," she said. "Let's check the other rooms backstage."

With all the noise and confusion, the girls were able to slip away easily

without being noticed. They hurried along the backstage corridor, and ran into the ladies' dressing room. Rachel looked in the lockers where the dancers had left their clothes, while Kirsty checked the cupboards and rummaged through the costumes. There was no sign of a goblin.

Next, they tried the office. Melodie flew out of Rachel's pocket to look under the desk, Rachel peered out of the window, and Kirsty opened all the drawers in the filing cabinet. There were papers and folders everywhere, but no goblin.

The three returned to the corridor feeling a little downhearted.

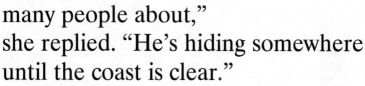

"Do you think he's already gone?" Rachel asked glumly.

Melodie shook her head, "Not with so many people about," she replied. "He's hiding somewhere until the coast is clear."

Suddenly Kirsty frowned. "I can hear something!" she exclaimed, listening hard. "Someone's playing the piano."

Now Rachel could hear it too, very faintly. "Maybe someone is practising in the music room," she suggested.

"But who would practise the piano

with a party going on?" asked Kirsty.

Rachel listened again. "Well, whoever it is, they certainly need the practice," she said, pulling a face. "It sounds terrible!"

Melodie's face lit up. "Only a goblin could play that badly!" she gasped, and immediately she zoomed off towards the sound. The girls ran after her. As they got closer to the music room, the jangling sound of the piano grew louder.

They found the door ajar, and peeped cautiously into the room. They could hear the terrible music clearly now, and they could even see the piano standing in the middle of the floor. But to their astonishment, there was nobody playing it!

Goblin Discovered

The girls stared at the piano in amazement. Even Melodie looked puzzled. But then Kirsty had an idea. "Maybe the goblin's hiding inside the piano!" she said. "And playing it from there."

"Let's go and look," Rachel suggested.

"No, I'll go," Kirsty replied. "Ballet

shoes are soft. If the goblin is in there, he won't hear me coming."

"Good idea," Rachel agreed. If the goblin was hiding in the piano, they didn't want to give him any warning.

Kirsty slipped through the open door and tiptoed over to the grand piano. Holding her breath, she carefully lifted the lid and peeked inside.

And there he was – a nasty-looking goblin, laughing gleefully and running up and down the piano strings, with Melodie's party bag swinging from one knobbly hand.

As he pranced, he sang to himself in a croaky voice: "I've got the party bag, I'm such a smarty. I'll take it to Jack Frost, and he'll throw a party!" Ever so gently, Kirsty lowered the piano lid. Then she turned to the door and nodded at Rachel and Melodie. "What do we do now?" Rachel whispered to Melodie. "How are we going to get your party bag back?"

35

Melodie frowned thoughtfully, as Rachel looked around the room. There was a set of drums not far from the grand piano, and on one of the drums lay a pair of cymbals. This gave Rachel a clever idea. "See those cymbals?" she said, pointing them out to Melodie. "Do you think you could lift one?"

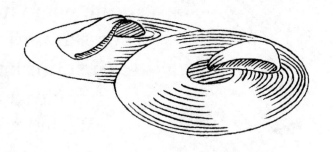

"I think so," Melodie replied, looking at Rachel curiously.

"Great! I'll take the other one," Rachel said.

"But how will you get there to pick it up?" Melodie asked. "If you walk across the room, the goblin might hear you."

"Not if I'm a fairy…" Rachel smiled. Melodie nodded and waved her wand. A shower of glittering fairy dust floated down around Rachel and she felt herself shrinking. By the time the sparkling dust had settled, Rachel was as tiny as Melodie herself. She fluttered her wings happily and flew around in a little circle. Then she set off across the music room, with

37

Melodie close behind.

The cymbals were heavy. Melodie and Rachel both had to struggle to lift them, but at last they managed it.

Quickly, they flew over to Kirsty, who had been watching them in bewilderment. Rachel whispered in Kirsty's ear so the goblin wouldn't hear.

"When I wink, open the lid of the piano," she said.

Kirsty nodded, wondering what Rachel was planning.

Rachel and Melodie held up the cymbals and hovered in the air, face to face. Then Rachel winked at Kirsty who immediately lifted the piano lid. At the very same moment, Rachel and Melodie rushed towards each other. And with a crash that shook the room, the cymbals clashed together right above the goblin's head!

A New
Problem

The goblin let out a loud scream,
clapped his hands over his ears and
dropped Melodie's party bag. "Oh,
what a dreadful noise!" he shrieked
in surprise. "My poor head hurts!"
And he leapt out of the piano and
ran from the room at top speed.

Rachel smiled to herself. The
cymbals had made a deafening
noise, she thought, but at least
she and Melodie had been ready
for it. She heard a smaller crash,
and looked round to see that
Melodie had dropped her cymbal
and swooped into the piano
to snatch up her party bag.

"Ooh, that was fun!" Melodie exclaimed. "The goblin escaped, but I've got my party bag and that's all that matters." She opened the bag and peeped inside. As she did so, some glittering, golden musical notes drifted out. "And it's still full of magic fairy dust," she declared happily.

At that moment, Kirsty heard footsteps in the corridor outside. "Someone's coming," she whispered. "Quick, you two, hide in the piano!"

Rachel dropped her cymbal with a clatter and flew to join Melodie inside the piano. Kirsty let the lid down quickly. She was just in time. The door to the room swung open, and Miss Kelly came in. "Hello, Kirsty, are you all right?" she asked anxiously. "Whatever was all that noise?"

Kirsty had to think very quickly.

"Er, I thought that there, um, might be another CD-player in this room," she explained. "I was looking for it when I knocked over the cymbals."

Miss Kelly laughed. "Well, we need you on stage now. I think we'll be able to start the ballet again in a minute. Melissa's dad is an electrician, and he's fixing the CD-player."

Kirsty frowned. Could a human electrician fix a machine that was broken by a goblin? She had a feeling that only fairy magic would get that CD-player working again. And she knew just who could help. But Melodie was stuck inside the piano with Rachel!

"I'll come in a moment, Miss Kelly," Kirsty said, thinking fast. "Some sequins fell off my costume. I just need to find them first."

"Your costume looks fine," the ballet teacher told her briskly. "A sequin or two makes no difference. Besides, there's no time to sew them back on, and we don't want to keep our audience waiting any longer."

Kirsty had no choice. Reluctantly, she followed Miss Kelly out of the music room, leaving Rachel and Melodie trapped inside the piano.

The Show Must Go On!

"Oh, no!" Rachel cried after Kirsty and Miss Kelly had gone. "Who knows how long we're going to be stuck in here now?"

Melodie laughed, a tinkling musical sound. "Don't worry, Rachel," she said. And with a wave of her magic wand, the piano lid

flew open in a shower of sparkling
fairy magic.

   Rachel and Melodie flew out.
As soon as Rachel reached the
ground, Melodie waved her wand
again and turned Rachel back
to her normal size. Then, clutching
her party bag tightly, Melodie hid
herself in Rachel's pocket. "We can
save the party now," she said
happily. "Let's go!"

As Rachel hurried out of the music room, she noticed that the squeaky, speeded-up music had stopped. She wondered if the spell had been broken when the goblin ran away. Or maybe Melissa's dad had fixed the CD-player somehow.

When she reached the stage, however, she saw a large group of people still gathered around the machine. Peering through the crowd, Rachel caught a glimpse of Melissa's dad with a screwdriver in one hand and a pair of pliers in the other. Miss Kelly and Kirsty were by his side.

"What's happening?" Melodie
hissed from Rachel's pocket.

"I think Melissa's dad took
the CD-player apart,"
Rachel whispered.

"There are bits of metal and
plastic all over the floor."

"Is he going
to put it back
together now?"
Melodie wanted
to know.

"I think so,"
Rachel murmured.
She edged
a little closer.

"I'm terribly sorry,"
the man was saying to
Miss Kelly. "I've repaired
CD-players before, but I've never
seen anything like this. I don't think
I can fix it."

"Do you think *you* can fix it?"
Rachel whispered to Melodie.

"Yes, I'm sure I can – with fairy
magic," Melodie answered. She
peeped out of Rachel's pocket and
her face fell. "But
not with all these
people around,"
she added.
"Someone
would see
me sprinkling
fairy dust over
the machine."

"Maybe I can
get everyone to
move away," Rachel
said thoughtfully. But though
she racked her brains, she couldn't
think of anything that would
make the people leave the
CD-player.

She looked round, hoping that a brilliant notion would pop into her head. And then she remembered the musical instruments in the wings on the other side of the stage, where she had first found Melodie.

They couldn't be seen from the CD-player, but when Rachel slipped across to the pile of instruments, she was pleased to see that there was nobody else about.

Gently, she lifted the little fairy out of her pocket. "Look," she said softly. "I've got an idea. Can you do anything with these musical instruments instead?"

Melodie smiled and clapped her hands.

"Yes, I can!" she exclaimed. "Is anyone looking?"

"No, we're out of sight round here," Rachel told her.

Quickly, Melodie fluttered over to the instruments and perched lightly on the violin. She took a handful of glittering musical notes from her party bag, and carefully sprinkled them over the violin's strings.

Then she flitted from instrument to instrument, throwing a few sparkling notes over each one. Finally, she waved her wand with an expert flourish.

At once, the bow that had been lying next to the violin floated into the air and began stroking the violin's strings.

The flute hovered, quivering, as soft, sweet sounds poured from it, while the strings of a harp were plucked by invisible fingers. Rachel heard the deep, low notes of a horn and watched in amazement as all the instruments began to play themselves.

From across the stage, Rachel heard Miss Kelly exclaim in surprise. "That's our ballet music!" she cried. "Where is it coming from?"

Rachel ran back to the group. "I found another CD-player," she told the ballet teacher. She caught Kirsty's eye and smiled. Rachel didn't have to tell her friend that there was fairy magic at work!

"Quickly, dancers take your places," Miss Kelly called. As the girls rushed onto the stage, the audience moved back to their seats.

Miss Kelly turned to Rachel. "Could you start the music from the beginning again, please?" she asked.

Rachel bit her lip. She wasn't sure that she could. What if Melodie had already gone back to Fairyland? Anxiously, she hurried back to the instruments, and then she smiled with relief. She should have known that Melodie wouldn't leave without saying goodbye. The fairy was still there, dancing around to the music, her white dress swirling around her.

"Can you start the music from the beginning?" Rachel asked her.

Melodie's wand fluttered and she threw a few more glittering musical notes into the air. The music stopped for an instant, and then began all over again.

As Kirsty and the others began to dance, Rachel and Melodie watched the performance from the wings.

"Oh, it's lovely!" Melodie exclaimed, copying the dancers' graceful arm movements.

"Just like it should be," Rachel agreed. The ballet went perfectly, and at the end the audience applauded wildly. The girls curtseyed, left the stage and went to join their proud parents. Except for Kirsty, who rushed over to the side of the stage.

"Thank you, Melodie," she said gratefully. "You saved our party."

"No, thank you," Melodie beamed. "Without you, there would be no music at the King and Queen's jubilee. Please keep an eye out for any more of Jack Frost's goblins."

"We will," Rachel and Kirsty promised together.

Melodie beamed. "Good luck," she said, and with a wave of her wand and a shower of twinkling lights, the fairy flew away.

Smiling happily, Rachel and Kirsty
made their way to the hall to enjoy
the rest of the party.

"I hope we meet more Party
Fairies," Rachel said.

"Oh, I'm sure we will," replied
Kirsty, and then she smiled. "As long
as we keep going to parties!" she
added.